This Book Belongs To:

The Muppet Babies live in a nursery
in a house on a street that is a lot like yours.
But they can travel anywhere anytime using a special power—
the power of the imagination.
Can you imagine what it would be like to go with them?
Join the Muppet Babies on this adventure and find out.

Weekly Reader Presents

If I Were Just Like Kermit

By H. B. Gilmour • Illustrated by Mary Bausman

Muppet Press/Marvel

This book is a presentation of
Weekly Reader Books.

Weekly Reader Books offers book clubs for children
from preschool through high school.

For further information write to:
Weekly Reader Books
4343 Equity Drive
Columbus, Ohio 43228

ISBN 0-87135-100-5

"Ah-ah-ah-choo!"
Baby Kermit had a cold. His nose was red. His eyes
looked bleary. Nanny said he had to stay in bed.

Baby Fozzie decided to cheer Kermit up with one of his jokes. "What's green and red and has to stay in bed?" he asked.

"Ah doh doh," said Kermit. He was trying to say, "I don't know."

"You are!" Baby Fozzie exclaimed. "You are green.
Your nose is red. And today you have to stay in bed."
    Kermit did not laugh. He just sighed and sneezed again.
    "*Ah-ah-ah-choo!* I deed sub rest." That meant,
"I need some rest." Then he rolled over and went
to sleep.

"I have failed," said Fozzie sadly as he shuffled away. "I tried to cheer up my friend Kermit, and instead, I put him to sleep."

He sat down on his rocking chair and rocked and thought.

"My friend Kermit is always kind and helpful and daring. He's brave and polite and clever, too. If I were sick, he would know exactly what to do to make me feel better."

Suddenly, Baby Fozzie snapped his fingers. "That's it!" he declared, throwing off his gloomy mood. "If I do just what Kermit would do, I can make him feel good! All I have to do is put myself in Kermit's place. I'll imagine what he would do if I were sick."

Fozzie closed his eyes. "Kermit is so kind. He would probably fix me a great big breakfast in bed. So that's what I'll do."

Fozzie imagined himself as Kermit. He imagined putting on a chef's hat and apron, and off he scurried to the kitchen.

Fozzie found some butter and six eggs. He dropped
three of the eggs on the floor and scrambled the others
in a frying pan. Then he put two nice thick slices of
bread in the toaster. He let them toast while he hunted
for jam.

The butter started to melt. The eggs and toast began to burn. Fozzie finally found the jam behind a pile of cans that toppled off a shelf.

"Oh dear!" cried Fozzie as the cans rolled across the floor. "I can 'bear-ly' see because of all the smoke. I'd better find a mop and pail to tidy up this awful mess. I have to be helpful because that is exactly what Kermit would do."

Determined to be as helpful as Kermit, Fozzie ran to the sink and turned on the water. Then off he went to find a pail. He hurried as fast as he could, but the water was faster than he was. By the time Baby Fozzie returned to the kitchen, there was enough water on the floor for a sea-faring bear to go sailing.

"What would Kermit—who is daring—do in a case like this?" Fozzie wondered, trying hard to stay afloat. "Why, Kermit would climb aboard the pail and sail off on an exciting adventure," he decided.

So he scrambled into the pail. The mop made a very fine oar. He peered through his spy glass in search of a distant shore.

All of a sudden, Baby Fozzie gulped, and he gasped, and he dropped his spy glass. He couldn't believe what he had seen. It was huge. It swam like a fish. Its tail was spiky and green.

The creature turned and splashed. The water churned and foamed. And daring Fozzie wished he were back in the nursery.

"What would Kermit do now?" Fozzie asked himself. "He would be brave. And he would also be polite."
So brave Fozzie sailed closer to the creature.
"Excuse me," he said politely to the beast, who was hidden behind the foam. "It's a pleasure to meet you. My name is Fozzie, and I'm trying my best to get home."

The creature's head poked out of the waves. Fozzie took one look and smiled. It was only a baby sea monster who had been taking a bubble bath. The little sea monster stared shyly at Fozzie. Its tail trembled with fright. Then it hiccupped a bouquet of bubbles and dove quickly out of sight.

Fozzie was starting to feel very hungry. "It must
be lunch time," he said to himself. "Now, what would
Kermit do? He is so clever. With all this water around,
he'd probably go fishing."

So Fozzie cast his mop overboard...

...into a school of tuna cans, through egg seashells and sailing pans, past floating toast and jam. Before long, he had caught a fine lunch.

It had been a lovely adventure, but Fozzie wished
he were back on dry land. "What would clever Kermit
do if he were tired of bobbing about in a pail?" Fozzie
wondered. "He certainly wouldn't fuss or shout.
Kermit would just reach overboard, pull the plug,
and let the water out!"

It seemed like a fine plan. So clever Fozzie reached overboard. But the pail tipped. Poor Fozzie fell out, and down he went. And down. And down.

Beneath the water, Fozzie thought he saw the plug.
He swam toward it with all his might.

The next thing Fozzie knew, he was staring at Nanny's shoes.

"Fozzie, why are you trying to swim on the nursery floor?" Nanny was asking. "Oh my! You've got a lump on your head. You must have fallen off your rocking chair. I'd better get you right into bed."

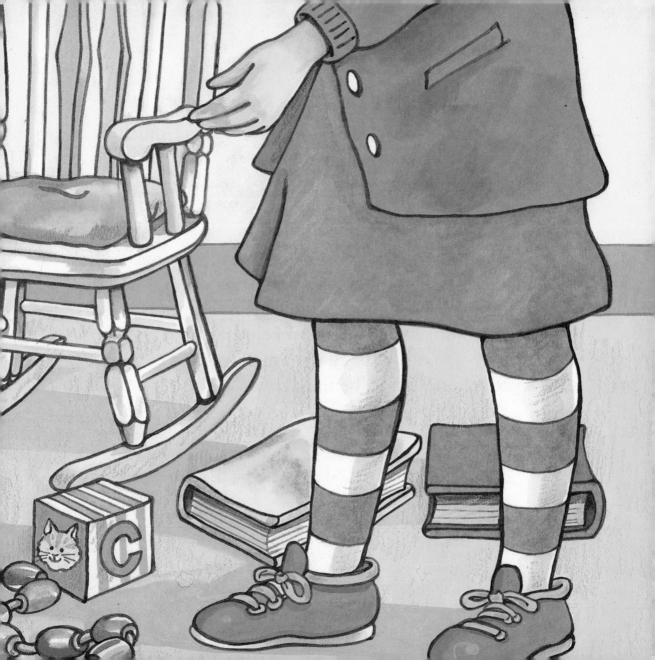

When Kermit woke up, he was feeling much better. He found Baby Fozzie lying next to him. Fozzie had an ice pack on his head.

"Fozzie, what happened to you?" Kermit wanted to know.

"Well, I thought that if I were just like you, I'd know how to make you feel better," Fozzie explained to his friend. "So I tried to be kind, helpful, and daring. And I tried to be brave, polite, and clever, too. But," said Fozzie, sighing, "I'm really much better at being myself than I am at being like you."

"Well, that's good," said Kermit, "because I like you just the way you are."

"You do?" asked Fozzie, smiling at last. "Well, then, how about a new joke? What's brown and very funny and has to stay in bed?" he asked, feeling like his old self again.

Kermit laughed. "My best friend," he said, "the one and only Fozzie!"